TO ETHAN

From Aunty YVONNE
Uncle John Sailer

Dec 25, 2007

Disney's
My Very First Winnie the Pooh™

A Bedtime Story
for Pooh

Adapted by
Cassandra Case

Illustrated by
John Kurtz

SCHOLASTIC INC.

New York Toronto London Auckland Sydney
Mexico City New Delhi Hong Kong Buenos Aires

Published by Scholastic Inc., 90 Old Sherman Turnpike, Danbury, CT 06816
by arrangement with Disney Licensed Publishing.

SCHOLASTIC and associated logos are trademarks
and/or registered trademarks of Scholastic Inc.

ISBN 0-7172-8897-8

Printed in the U.S.A.

Each morning, the sun peeked
into Pooh's window and woke
him up. Pooh knew then it was
time to choose a pot of honey and
have a nice breakfast.

But this morning was different.
Pooh had not slept one wink all
night! He sat on the edge of his
bed and sighed.

"If breakfast is what you eat when you wake up,
what do you do if you haven't been to sleep?
Think, think, think."

To give his thoughts more room, Pooh got
dressed and went out into the Hundred-Acre Wood.

Pooh walked for a while, but he still didn't know what to do.

"I'll sit on this tree stump," Pooh said to himself. "Perhaps a good idea will come to me."

But what came along instead was Tigger.

"Pooh Boy," cried Tigger, "you look as if you losted a friend! But I'm right here—see?"

"I'm trying to get an idea," replied Pooh.

"Oh! I get lotsa ideas at breakfast!" said Tigger. "Let's go eat breakfast!"

"I can't," sighed Pooh.

"Winnie the Pooh can't have breakfast?" said Tigger in surprise. "Why not?"

"Because breakfast is what you have after a night's sleep," Pooh explained, "and I haven't had any sleep yet."

"No sleep! What happened?" asked Tigger.

"I'm not sure," Pooh replied. "My bed was comfy and cozy . . . I'd had a good-night smackerel, so there was no rumbly in my tummy to keep me awake . . . ."

"Ah-*ha*," interrupted Tigger. "A gigantical, growly-type aminal outside your window kept you awake, right?"

"No," Pooh replied. "Actually, I think it was a little, chirpy-type amina—er, animal *inside* my window that kept me up. I believe it was a cricket."

"Wow!" said Tigger. "I couldn't've heard my bedtime story if so many nosy noises were happenin' inside my house."

"Bedtime story?" Pooh asked. "I didn't hear any bedtime story."

"Hoo-hoo-hoo, that's it!" Tigger shouted, bouncing Pooh in his excitement. "No wonder you stayed awake! Nobody read you a bedtime story!"

With Tigger standing on it, Pooh's hungry tummy made a rumbly sound.

Pooh thought hard.

"You mean, if someone tells me a story that puts me to sleep, then I can wake up for breakfast?" asked Pooh.

"Sure!" Tigger replied.

"But where can I find a bedtime story in the morning?" Pooh sighed. "Oh, bother!"

"Don't you worry, Buddy Boy," cried Tigger. "I've got a doozy of a story for you!"

So Tigger told Pooh an exciting story about the time when he bounced higher than Owl can fly.

When the story ended, Pooh was quiet. He was wondering if he should believe the story or not.

"Pooh?" whispered Tigger. "Are you asleep yet?"

"I don't think so," Pooh whispered back.

"Well, then," said Tigger, "what do you think about vegebibbles?"

Pooh opened his mouth to say "What do you mean?" but a large yawn came out instead.

"I thought so!" said Tigger. "Let's go ask Rabbit to tell you about his garden. *That* should put you to sleep!"

$\mathcal{M}$inutes later, they were sitting at a table in Rabbit's house.

"A story about vegetables?" said Rabbit. "I'm not good at stories. I don't finish them."

"Why not?" asked Pooh.

"I fall asleep," answered Rabbit.

"Hoo-hoo-hoo!" cried Tigger. "That's just the very kind of story Pooh needs to hear!"

So Rabbit *began* a story about a garden. But then he got talking about all the different kinds of seeds. There were *so* many of them! It was too confusing for a bear of very little brain.

Pooh stopped listening to Rabbit. He started imagining which pot of honey he would eat when he woke up for breakfast. He had decided just which one it would be when he noticed that it was very quiet. He looked around. Rabbit and Tigger were both fast asleep!

"Oh, bother!" sighed Pooh. "Why didn't I listen? Now where am I going to find a story to put *me* to sleep?" Then Pooh thought of Piglet.

"When I'm with Piglet, nothing is quite as bad as it seems," he said.

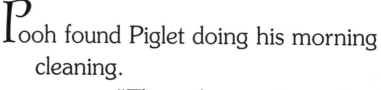

Pooh found Piglet doing his morning cleaning.

"The only story I can think of," said Piglet, "is that one you made up about me."

"*I* made up a story?" said Pooh in surprise.

"Yes," Piglet replied. "That hum you made up when I was feeling very, very small. Remember?"

"Would you tell it to me now?" asked Pooh.

"I-i-it's *your* hum, Pooh." Piglet's ears twitched uncertainly. "I only remember *some* of the story. And I forgot the rhymes."

"Well, never mind," Pooh sighed. "I forgot, too."

"Why not go and see Owl?" suggested Piglet. "He's very wise. And anyway, he always makes me feel sleepy when he gets talking about everything he knows. Maybe he can help you."

"What a good idea, Piglet!" said Pooh with a chuckle. "Yes, Owl does have a way of talking on and on! I'll go see him right now!"

But Owl was getting ready to go out.

"Please don't go yet, Owl," said Pooh. "Would you very kindly tell me a bedtime story before you leave? I need to go to sleep so I can wake up and have my breakfast."

"Woooo!" Owl hooted. "A most complicated conundrum, if *ever* I heard one! I *am* sorry, dear Pooh, but I cannot possibly stay. I must fly! Some other time, perhaps?"

And with a wave of his wing, Owl swooped off over the Hundred-Acre Wood.

"What shall I do *now*?" Pooh wondered out loud as he headed away from Owl's house.

"That depends," came Eeyore's voice from beside the path. "What *were* you doing, Pooh?"

"Oh, Eeyore!" cried Pooh. "Am I glad to see you!"

"You *are*?" Eeyore said in surprise.

"Yes, I am!" replied Pooh. "I was looking for someone to tell me a bedtime story to put me to sleep. I didn't sleep last night, you see, so I couldn't wake up for breakfast—because I was already awake—and now I don't know what to do."

Eeyore thought this over as he munched on a thistle. Pooh watched. His poor tummy was feeling very rumbly.

"It seems to me," said Eeyore slowly, "that *if* someone—such as you, Pooh—had a problem such as this one—a *mother* might be a good person to ask about it."

"Oh!" Pooh exclaimed. "Do you think Kanga can help?"

"I wouldn't be surprised," said Eeyore, giving Pooh a friendly nudge. "Just go and ask her."

"Of course I can help," said Kanga, smiling. She sat down in her rocking chair and took Pooh onto her lap.

"Once upon a time," Kanga began, "there lived a bear who was very, very tired, indeed."

"Yes," Pooh yawned, "very tired, I'm sure."

"He was *so* tired," Kanga went on, "that . . ."

"Zzzzz," Pooh snored. He was so comfy and cozy that he had fallen asleep at last!

A little later, Tigger, Rabbit, Piglet, Owl, Roo, Gopher, and Eeyore tiptoed in. Kanga held a finger to her lips as they quietly set out a wonderful breakfast to share with Pooh—just as soon as he woke up!